Maxwell

D0126875

Aladdin Books
Macmillan Publishing Company
866 Third Avenue, New York, NY 10022
Collier Macmillan Canada, Inc.

First Aladdin Books edition 1988
Printed in the United States of America

A hardcover edition of *The Pearl* is available from Margaret
K. McElderry Books, Macmillan Publishing Company.

10 9 8 7 6 5 4 3 2 1

Library of Congress Cataloging-in-Publication Data

Heine, Helme.
[Perle. English]
The pearl / Helme Heine.—1st Aladdin books ed.
p.   cm.
Translation of: Die Perle.
Summary: Beaver's excitement at finding a mussel that doubtless
contains a pearl is tempered by the realization that such a treasure
could stir the greed of his friends, causing a chain of
environmentally disastrous events.
ISBN 0-689-71262-6 (pbk.)
[1. Greed—Fiction.   2. Environmental protection—Fiction.
3. Beavers—Fiction.   4. Forest animals—Fiction.]   I. Title.
PZ7.H3678Pe   1988
[E]—dc19   88-3220   CIP   AC

Helme Heine

The
Pearl

ALADDIN BOOKS
Macmillan Publishing Company
New York

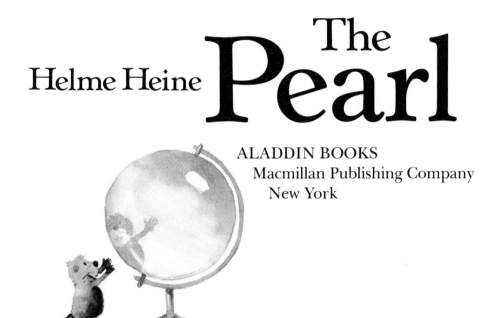

The little boat drifted slowly away but Beaver did not notice it. He could think of nothing but the shell he had found while playing in the lake.

He looked at it from every angle, sniffing it thoroughly.
There was no doubt about it: it was a freshwater
pearl mussel.

Beaver had found a treasure—or at least a treasure chest.
Not for one moment did he doubt that there was a pearl inside
the mussel. Why else would it be called a pearl mussel? Overcome
with happiness, Beaver hugged the mussel to his heart, closed his eyes
and began to dream . . .

He dreamed that his friends were looking at him in astonishment. "Beaver has found the greatest treasure in the forest," they said to themselves, and they were filled with envy.

When they asked where the pearl had come from, Beaver stammered: "From the forest. Under a toadstool. A long way from here. A very long way."

His friends did not believe him. "Pearls are found in
mussels in the lake," they said. "Not in the forest."
Leaving him, they began to search the shallow waters
near the shore.

"This is my lake!" screamed Beaver. "I built the dam.
The mussels are mine!"

At first none of his friends paid the slightest attention to him. But finally the bear—in a furious temper—growled: "And what did you use to build your dam? You used trees. And they came from our forest. Therefore, the lake and all the mussels we find are ours."

There was nothing Beaver could do but watch helplessly
while more and more animals joined in the
treasure hunt.

Many of the animals could not swim or even paddle.
They destroyed Beaver's dam so all the water ran out.
Then they, too, searched frantically for mussels.

Up to their knees in sand and mud, the treasure hunters
squabbled over every mussel, hurling insults and
mud at each other.

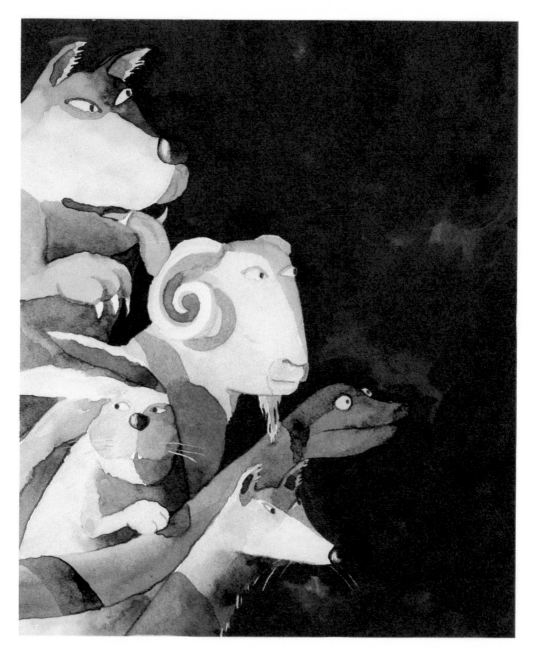

As darkness fell, the treasure hunters built a huge bonfire.

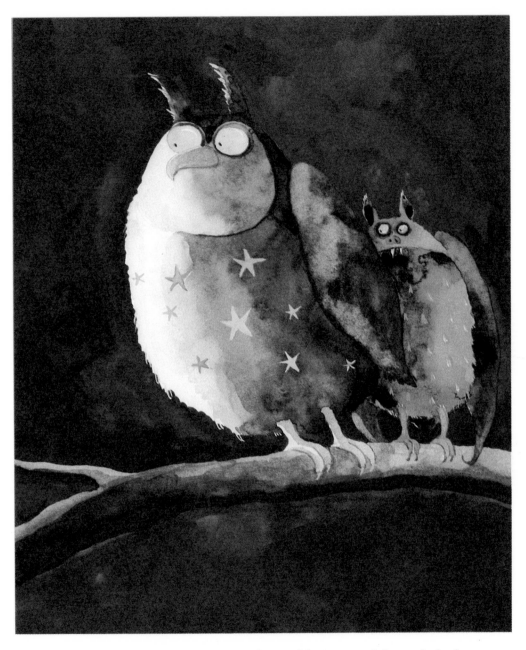

They were afraid that owls and bats would steal their
mussels. Exhausted though they were, they kept
watch all night.

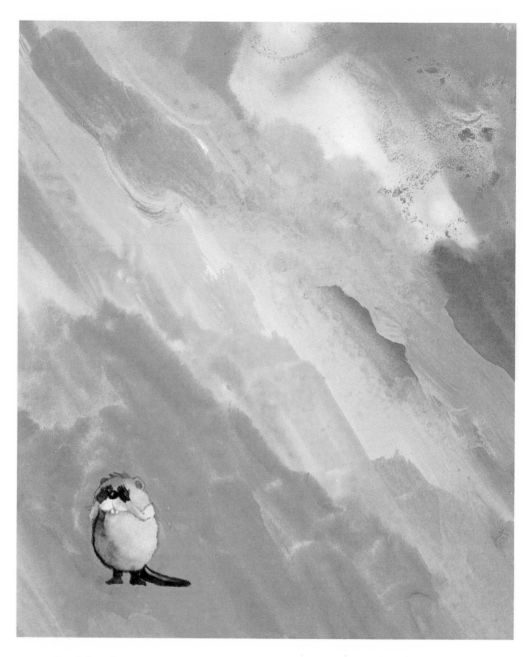

Suddenly, a gust of wind showered the forest with sparks
and flames from the bonfire. Beaver's house was soon
ablaze—and there was no water in the lake with which
to fight the fire. It destroyed everything, even Beaver
and the pearl . . .

. . . Beaver awoke terrified from his horrible dream.
While he thought about it he looked at the mussel he had
not yet opened.

Picking it up, he hurled the mussel as far as he could
into the lake.

It skimmed the surface, bouncing seven times before it sank, something he had never managed to do before.

Then, happy once more, Beaver plunged into the water and swam after his little boat. It had nearly reached the other side of the lake where all his friends were waiting for him to come and play.